CIRCUS ★ TRAIN

⁺ BY ⁺

Jennifer Cole Judd

⁺ ILLUSTRATED BY ⁺

Melanie Matthews

two lions

To Anna, whose wide-eyed wonder put this train in motion.
And to the rest of my crew, who make life as entertaining as a three-ring circus.
—J. C. J.

For Pip, my little circus clown.
—M. M.

two lions

Text copyright © 2015 Jennifer Cole Judd
Illustrations copyright © 2015 Melanie Matthews
All rights reserved.

Published by Two Lions, New York

www.apub.com

LCCN: 2014944827
ISBN-13: 9781477826348 | ISBN-10: 1477826343

The illustrations were rendered in digital media.
Book design by Abby Kuperstock

Printed in China
First Edition

CIRCUS TRAIN spills over the hills.

Along the road
crews unload.
Workers **ZOOM**.
Tents bloom.

Clowns **PAINT** faces,
straighten laces.
Day grows warm.
Long lines form.

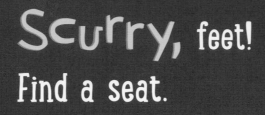

Scurry, feet!
Find a seat.

Spotlights glow—
let's start the . . .

Elephants dancing.
Poodles prancing.
TUMBLING, twirling,
flags unfurling.

Diving, dipping, trapeze flipping.

Oohs and aahs.
Applause! APPLAUSE!

Tigers, horses
weave through courses.

Vendors handy—

"Cotton candy!"

Fire on the grounds!
Here come the CLOWNS!

Ringmaster cries,
"Look out! Cream pies!"

Tightrope wire,
cannon fire.

The crowds roar,
"ENCORE!
ENCORE!"

A floor of roses,
circus closes.

Crews load cars
beneath the stars.
Train lights glow.
Time to go.

Circus train spills
over the hills.